Dog for a Day

Dick Gackenbach

Clarion Books
NEW YORK

Clarion Books

a Houghton Mifflin Company imprint

215 Park Avenue South, New York, NY 10003

Copyright © 1987 by Dick Gackenbach

Printed in Hong Kong

Library of Congress Cataloging-in-Publication Data

Gackenbach, Dick.

Dog for a day.

Summary: After transforming a football into a toaster

and a cat into a canary, Sidney's new invention creates

unexpected problems by changing Sidney into his dog.

and his dog into Sidney.

[1. Inventions—Fiction.   2. Dogs—Fiction]

I. Title.

PZ7.G117Dp 1987   [E]   86-17514

ISBN 0-89919-452-4 PA ISBN 0-89919-851-1

DNP   10   9

For Liz and Larry Miller

Sidney was in second grade and he was very smart. Some people called Sidney a genius. He was good at inventing things.

One day Sidney invented something he called a Changing Box. How it worked was Sidney's secret. Whatever he put in the box would change into something else when Sidney pressed a button.

Sidney changed his baby sister into a lamp, but he had to change her back again when his mother got upset.

He changed a football into a toaster, the cat into the canary, and the canary into the cat. Around Sidney's house, no one knew what was what any more.

One morning Sidney decided to change
himself. "I'm tired of being Sidney," he said.
Sidney thought it might be fun to be a
dog for a while. So he took his dog, Wally, and
together they crawled into the Changing Box.

"What a good time
I'll have being a dog!"
chuckled Sidney.
Wally whimpered.

In a few minutes, Sidney came out of the box looking like Wally, his dog. And Wally came out looking like Sidney.

"Super!" said Sidney. He was pleased with the change.

Wally sniffed at his bowl to make sure his food was still there. Then he lay down on his pillow for a morning nap.

When it was time for school, Sidney put his books in his mouth, sneaked out of the house, and headed for the school bus. But when he tried to get on the bus, the door closed in his face.

"No dogs allowed," shouted the driver.

"But I'm Sidney," said Sidney.

"Sidney doesn't have floppy ears," replied the driver as he pulled away.

So Sidney had to walk to school.

At school, Sidney took his usual seat. His teacher, Mrs. Miller, told him he had to leave. "No dogs in school," she said. "OUT!"

"But I'm Sidney," said Sidney.

"Sidney doesn't have a cold wet nose," said
Mrs. Miller as she pushed him out the door.

There was nothing Sidney could do but sit on the steps until school was over. He was waiting for his friends to come out to play baseball.

But his friends wouldn't let Sidney join the game.

"No dogs on our team," they told him.

"But I'm Sidney," said Sidney.

"Sidney doesn't have fleas," they said.

Back at home, Wally the dog was having
problems, too. Why was Sidney's mother telling
him to go to school?

Wally couldn't even take a nap. "Sidney,"
Sidney's mother said, "Get off of Wally's
pillow."

Wally couldn't eat his *Doggie Delights*, either. "Sidney, stop eating from Wally's bowl," Sidney's father yelled.

Wally whined. It was enough to make a dog leave home!

Meanwhile, Sidney tried to go to the movies, but he couldn't buy a ticket. "No dogs allowed in the theater," he was told.

Then Sidney went to the ice cream store. The owner of the store gave him some vanilla, but Sidney had to eat it from a dish on the floor. "Sorry," the man said. "We don't let dogs sit at the counter."

"It's no fun being a dog," Sidney complained. "I'm going home and change back to being a boy again."

But Sidney's troubles got even worse on his way home. First, a gang of bully dogs attacked him. Then five stray cats chased him up a light pole.

And if that wasn't enough, Sidney was stopped by a dogcatcher.

"Ah," said the dogcatcher. "No collar and no license, I see. It's the dog pound for you!"

Sidney gulped. If he went to the dog pound, he might remain a dog forever.

Before the dogcatcher could put the net over him, Sidney slipped through the man's legs and ran home as fast as all four paws could take him.

Sidney slammed the front door behind
him. Without wasting a second, he shoved
Wally off his pillow and into the Changing Box.

When they came out, Sidney was Sidney again, and Wally was Wally. Both boy and dog were happy to be themselves once more.

"Sometimes," Sidney said, "things are better left the way they are."

"WOOF!" Wally agreed.

That evening, Sidney took the Changing Box apart and tossed it away.

"Now," he said. "What will I think of next?"